# A VISIT TO

# Italy

## REVISED AND UPDATED

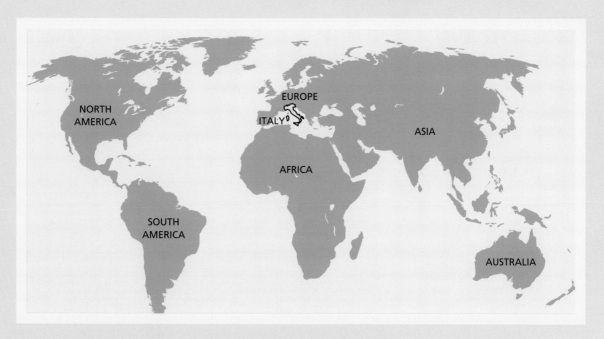

# Rachael Bell

Heinemann Library
Chicago, Illinois

Designed by Heinemann Library
Printed in the United States of America in
Eau Claire, Wisconsin.

051614
0082500P


**Library of Congress Cataloging-in-Publication Data**
Bell, Rachael,  1972-
           A visit to Italy / Rachael Bell
p.      cm. – (A visit to)
Includes Bibliographical references and index.
Summary: Introduces the land, landmarks, homes, food, clothes, work, transportation, language, school, recreation, and culture of Italy.
ISBN 978-1-4329-1270-3 (lib.bdg.) ISBN 978-1-4329-1289-5 (pbk.)
1.     Italy—Juvenile literature. [1. Italy.]  I. Title
II. Title: Italy. III. Series
DG417.B45     1999                                              99-18085
945—dc21

**Acknowledgements**
The publishers would like to thank the following for permission to reproduce photographs: © Axel Poignant Archive p. **29** (Ali Reale); © Colorific p. **22** (David Levenson/Black Star); © Colorsport p. **24**; © Corbis pp. **13** (Reuters/Tony Gentile), **22** (Silvia Morara); © Hutchison Library pp. **23** (J. Davey), **25** (Isabella Tree); © J. Allan Cash pp. **9**, **17**, **21**; © Katz Pictures p. **14** (A. Tosatto); © Performing Arts Library p. **28** (Gianfranco Fainello); © Photolibrary p. **5** (PhotoDisc/John A. Rizzo); © Punchstock p. **12** (Digital Vision); © Robert Francis p. **18**; © Robert Harding Picture Library/Mike Newton pp. **12**, **20**; © Stock Market p. **10**; © Telegraph Color Library  pp. **6** (J. Sims), **8**, **16** (J. Sims); © Tony Stone p. **11** (Joe Cornish); © Trevor Clifford p. **16**; © Trip pp. **7** (R. Cracknell), **15** (P. Nicholas), **20** (W. Jacobs), **26** (W. Jacobs), **27** (H. Rogers).

Cover photograph reproduced with permission of © Lonely Planet Images (Glenn Beanland).

Our thanks to Nick Lapthorn for his comments in the preparation of this book.

Every effort has been made to contact copyright holders of any material reproduced in this book. Any omissions will be rectified in subsequent printings if notice is given to the publishers.

# Contents

Any words appearing in bold, **like this**, are explained in the Glossary.

# Italy

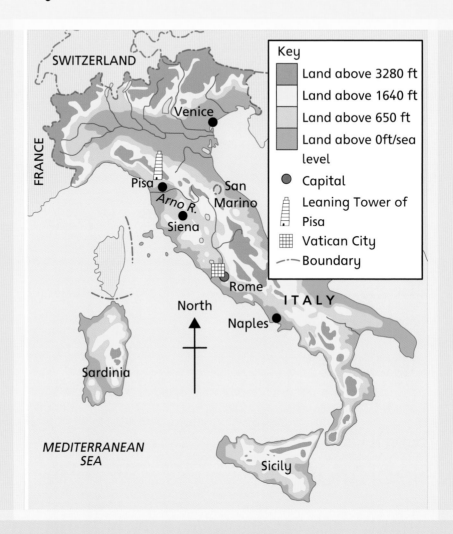

Key
- Land above 3280 ft
- Land above 1640 ft
- Land above 650 ft
- Land above 0ft/sea level
- ● Capital
- Leaning Tower of Pisa
- Vatican City
- Boundary

SWITZERLAND

FRANCE

Venice

Pisa
Arno R.
San Marino
Siena

Rome
ITALY
North
Naples

Sardinia

MEDITERRANEAN SEA

Sicily

Italy is in southern **Europe**. On a map it looks like a boot sticking out into the Mediterranean Sea. Sicily and Sardinia are islands that are part of Italy.

About 150 years ago, different areas joined up to make Italy. There are still two places inside Italy that are not part of it. They are the Vatican City and San Marino.

The Arno River flows through the city of Florence.

5

# Land

Most of the land in Italy is mountains or hills. These have only thin soil. Farming is difficult here. Many plants cannot grow in thin soil.

In the south of Italy it can get very hot and there is very little rain. The highest mountains are in the north.

Some mountains have snow on them all year round.

7

# Landmarks

One of Italy's most famous buildings is the Leaning Tower of Pisa. It is over 800 years old. There are 294 steps to the top of the tower.

This statue was carved over 500 years ago by a sculptor called Michelangelo.

The Vatican City is like a small, separate country inside Rome. It is the home of the **Pope**. There are lots of beautiful works of art by famous artists here.

# Homes

Most people in Italy live in towns or cities. The city of Naples grew up around a busy **port**. People left the countryside to come to Naples for work.

In the country, most houses have a small area of land around them. People can grow food for themselves or to sell.

# Food

Many families enjoy eating together. For lunch they might eat cold meats with salad, **pasta**, bread, and cheese.

This pizzeria is in Rome.

Many delicious foods come from Italy. Pizzas first came from Naples but now most towns have a pizzeria. You can watch the pizzas being made there.

# Clothes

Many famous fashion designers come from Italy. Young people usually wear casual or sports clothes.

In the countryside, people wear simple clothes. Some of the older Italian people always wear black.

# Work

This farm in Sicily is growing oranges.

Some people work on farms. They grow wheat, fruit, and vegetables. Many workplaces close in the middle of the day because it is so hot.

In central and southern Italy many people work in shops and offices. Most of Italy's **factories**, where they make **products** such as cars or engines, are in the north.

# Transportation

Italy has good roads and **toll** motorways. It also has a very good train service. There are **ports** and airports, too. Many young people ride **scooters**.

Boats called gondolas are an unusual way to get from place to place. People use them to get around the city of Venice, which has **canals** instead of streets.

# Language

Italy's **official language** is Italian. But different **regions** have their own **dialect**. The words in Italian are based on an old language called Latin.

The other main language is Sardinian. This is spoken by people on the island of Sardinia. Sardinian people also have special clothes for festivals.

# School

Primary school is for 6 to 11 year olds. School starts at 8:30 in the morning and finishes at about 1:00 in the afternoon. Pupils go to school six days a week.

Middle school is for 11 to 14 year olds.

The school day in middle school is longer and pupils usually have sports after school hours. Some pupils go to high school.

# Free Time

Most Italians love soccer. People of all ages talk about it and play it. There are big matches on Sunday afternoons.

In the early evening it is usual for people to meet up and walk around the main square or street in their town.

Walking around the square is called *passeggiata* (pa-se-jeeah-ta).

# Celebrations

Every town in Italy has at least one festival. People take the day off work or school to watch a **procession** through the town.

The horse race in Siena is called the Palio.

On July 2 and August 16 there is a bareback horse race in Siena. Before the race, people parade around the main square in costumes.

# The Arts

Italy has many **opera** singers and many Italians enjoy opera. Some of the operas take place in the **stadiums** built by the **ancient Romans**.

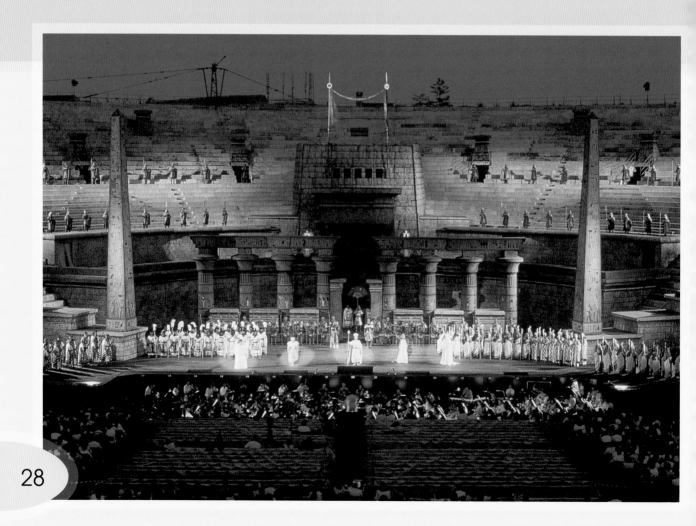

There are shows of puppets on strings as well as hand puppets.

Puppet shows started in Italy hundreds of years ago. Today, puppet shows are still very popular in Sicily.

# Fact File

**Name**       The full name for Italy is the Italian Republic.

**Capital**    The **capital** of Italy is Rome.

**Language**   Italy has two **official languages**: Italian and Sardinian.

**Population** About 59 million people live in italy.

**Money**      Italian money is called euros.

**Religions**  Almost all Italians are brought up as Roman Catholic.

**Products**   Italy produces wheat, vegetables, olives, wine, machinery, and clothes.

## Words you can learn

| | |
|---|---|
| uno (oono) | one |
| due (doo-ay) | two |
| tre (tray) | three |
| si (see) | yes |
| non (noh) | no |
| buon giorno (bwon JORno) | hello |
| arrivederci (a-ree-va-DAIR-chee) | goodbye |
| per favore (per-faVOR-eh) | please |
| grazie (graht-zee-ay) | thank you |

# Glossary

**ancient Romans** the people who ruled most of Europe from Rome, over 2000 years ago

**canal** river dug by people

**capital** city where the government is based

**dialect** language spoken by people in one area

**Europe** the continent north of the Mediterranean Sea

**factory** building where things are made in large amounts

**official language** language that is used by the government and that is used in education

**opera** a play with music and singing

**pasta** a kind of dough that is made from flour and is cooked in boiling water. Spaghetti is a type of pasta.

**Pope** the head of the Roman Catholic Church

**port** place where ships pick up and drop off the goods they are carrying

**procession** a group of people walking along behind each other and often wearing costumes

**product** a thing which is grown, taken from the earth, made by hand or made in a factory

**region** area or part of a country

**scooter** small-wheeled motorbike

**stadium** large sports ground surrounded by seats

**toll** payment you have to make in some places for driving on the motorway

# Index